MORRIS MacMILLIPEDE
The Toast of Brussels Sprout

MORRIS MacMILLIPEDE
The Toast of Brussels Sprout

MICK FITZMAURICE
ILLUSTRATED BY SATOSHI KITAMURA

Andersen Press
London

This edition published in 2010 by
Andersen Press Limited
20 Vauxhall Bridge Road
London SW1V 2SA
www.andersenpress.co.uk

First published in 1994 by Andersen Press Limited.

British Library Cataloguing in Publication Data available.

ISBN 978 184 270 862 0

Mixed Sources
Product group from well-managed
forests and other controlled sources
www.fsc.org Cert no. TT-COC-0002227
© 1996 Forest Stewardship Council
FSC

Printed and bound in Great Britain by CPI Bookmarque,
Croydon CR0 4TD

Chapter One

Morris Macmillipede is eight years old and has 42 pairs of legs. And 42 pairs of feet. And 42 pairs of trainers.

His mother, Millicent Macmillipede, reads the Nine o'Clock News on Bee Bee Bee Television. His father, Mackintosh M. Macmillipede, is a policeman. He arrested the Ghastly Greenfly Gang and the Big Bad Bed Bug Brothers. Thanks to Mackintosh M., they're safely locked up in Woodworm Scrubs prison.

The Macmillipedes live at 26, Rhubarb Road in Brussels Sprout, the biggest insect city in Bell Lane Market. They have a four-bedroomed house made entirely of cabbage leaves. The problem is, they love the taste of cabbage, and they're forever nibbling at the walls and floors and ceilings. Mackintosh M. is always patching up holes to stop the rain coming in.

Chapter Two

Brussels Sprout is a wonderful place for a young millipede. There are playgrounds with celery slides and radish roundabouts, and lovely, smelly gutters everywhere. On Saturdays, everyone goes to watch Earwig Rovers, the champions of the Football League.

But you'll never find Morris at the football match or playing with the other boys. For Morris has a secret.

It all started when he went with his school to see the Royal Insect Ballet. His friends were

bored, but Morris loved the theatre and the dancing and the costumes and the romantic music of Flykovsky. And most of all, he loved the ballerina, Dame Gossamer Spider.

"She's so beautiful," he sighed. "I wish I could share her web."

Ever since that day, he's wanted to be a ballet dancer. He hasn't told his friends or his brothers, for he knows they'd laugh at him. But when the other boys go out to play, Morris stays at home and dances with his reflection in the mirror.

Chapter Three

But Morris had to tell *someone* about his dream or he'd explode. He decided to tell his mother; surely she wouldn't laugh? But Mrs Macmillipede *did* laugh.

"A ballet dancer!" she said. "Whatever will you think of next?" She shook Morris's head to make sure his brain wasn't broken, then laughed all the way downstairs to cook the dinner.

A tear rolled down Morris's cheek and fell onto the carpet. His dream would never come true; he'd never dance with Dame Gossamer. If his own mother laughed at him, who would take him seriously?

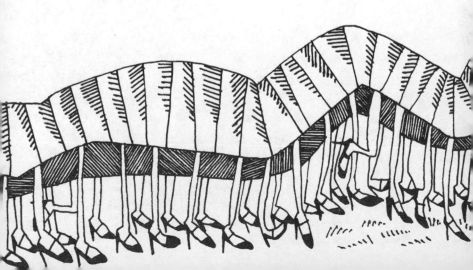

Chapter Four

Morris crept out of his house and wandered sadly through the streets of Brussels Sprout. The afternoon slipped by and the sky grew dark. The Money Spiders went home from their offices, rushing to catch their trains.

"Stocks and shares," they said to each other. "Stocks and shares."

Morris shivered as the icy wind sliced through his thin pullover. He was hungry, but all he had in his pocket was a piece of beetroot-flavoured bubblegum. He sat on a wall and chewed until the gum was soft and tasteless. Then he blew a broken-hearted little bubble.

Would his mother have missed him yet, he wondered? He felt so sad and lonely, he burst into tears.

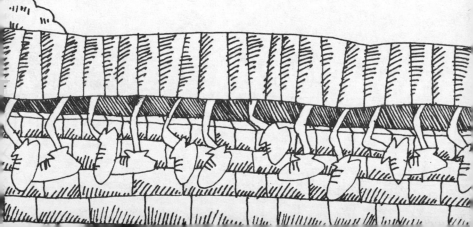

Chapter Five

"Well!" said a gruff voice. "You *do* seem sorry for yourself."

Morris looked up. There stood an old Stag Beetle with a long, grey beard.

"If you were me," sniffed Morris, "you'd feel sorry too."

"And why's that?" asked the old man, puffing at his pipe.

"Well . . ." Morris began, then told him all about his broken dream.

"Most unusual," said the Stag Beetle when Morris had finished. "Most boys want to play for Earwig Rovers or the England Crickets team.

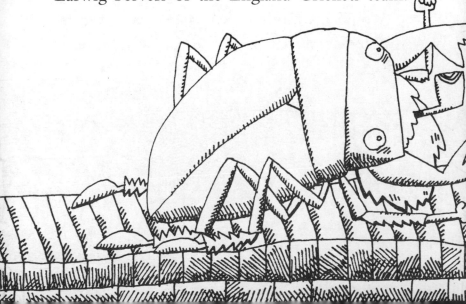

All the young Beetles want to be pop stars. But you want to be a ballet dancer."

"Yes," said Morris in a small voice, hoping the old man wouldn't laugh. And he didn't.

"If you want to do something badly enough," said the Beetle, "you shouldn't care what other people think. And if at first you don't succeed, what must you do?"

"Try and try and try again," Morris whispered.

"Quite right," said the Beetle. Then he puffed once more at his pipe and shuffled away into the darkness.

Chapter Six

By the time Morris arrived home, he was feeling much happier. He *wouldn't* care what people thought; he *would* try and try and try again.

He had a tasty tea of stale sprouts and squashed tomato, then lay on his bed thinking. Somehow he had to pay for ballet shoes and dancing lessons; but there was nothing in his money-box except a mouldy piece of chocolate.

What could he do? He stared sadly at his wallpaper with its rows of round, blue turnips. Then suddenly he had an idea. Round ... paper ... It was such a good idea that he set his alarm for five o'clock, nestled his 84 feet on his 84 hot-water bottles and fell fast asleep.

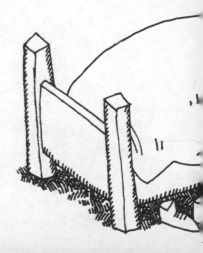

Chapter Seven

At five o'clock the next morning, Morris dragged himself out of bed. It was dark and cold, and last night's wonderful idea didn't seem so wonderful now. But he wasn't going to give up.

He put on four pullovers and ran along Rhubarb Road to Mr O'Wasp's newsagent's shop. He'd seen the notice in the window yesterday.

SMART
BOY OR GIRL
WANTED FOR
NEWSPAPER ROUND

Morris pushed open the door. It was lovely and warm inside.

"If it izzzzn't young Morrizzzz," buzzed Mr O'Wasp. "And what can I do for you?"

"I'd like a job," said Morris.

Chapter Eight

He began work the next morning at half past five. It was damp and misty, and the bag of newspapers felt almost as heavy as himself. But he didn't complain; he just trudged round Brussels Sprout delivering *The News of the Worm* and *The Daily Snail*, thinking about Dame Gossamer.

It all seemed worthwhile on Saturday when Mr O'Wasp put ten pound coins into his hand. "Here are your wagezzzz," he buzzed, and Morris ran home and put the money in an old biscuit tin under his bed.

In the months that followed, Morris often wanted to turn over and go back to sleep when his alarm clock went off. But he'd reach under the bed and feel the biscuit tin growing heavier and heavier, and he'd drag himself out into the cold streets once again.

On New Year's Eve, he decided it was time to count his savings. He tipped the coins onto his carpet . . . there was £120. It was enough! Tomorrow he'd go shopping!

Chapter Nine

Clutching the biscuit tin, Morris pressed his nose against the shop window. His eyes were wide with excitement as he stared, not at toy soldiers or train sets, but at a row of dainty, pink ballet shoes.

He pushed open the heavy door and went inside. Dark, wooden shelves rose to the ceiling; faded photographs of ballet dancers crowded the walls. Everything in the shop seemed old, not least the owner, a Great-Great-Grand-Daddy Long Legs, who shuffled slowly from the back room.

"Can I help you?" he wheezed, looking at Morris over his gold-rimmed spectacles.

"I'd like 42 pairs of ballet shoes, please," said Morris.

"That's enough for a whole school!" exclaimed the old Daddy Long Legs.

"But they're all for me," said Morris, pointing to his 84 feet.

The Great-Great-Grand-Daddy Long Legs counted out the shoes.

"There, young man. That'll be £84."

Morris gave him the money, then ran home and went straight upstairs to his bedroom. It took ages to tie up all the laces, but finally he was ready. He looked at himself in the mirror and could hardly believe what he saw.

"Morris Macmillipede," he whispered proudly, "you're a real ballet dancer now."

Chapter Ten

The Ballet School stood halfway along Onion Avenue. Morris went nervously inside and found a door marked

MADAME BUTTERFLY

He pushed open the door. Madame Butterfly lay on a sofa dressed in flowing silks of red and blue and yellow.

"I'd like to join your ballet class," said Morris timidly.

"Well!" she said. "A millipede in a ballet class! Whatever next!"

For a moment, Morris thought she might be laughing at him; but she took his money seriously and sent him off to get changed.

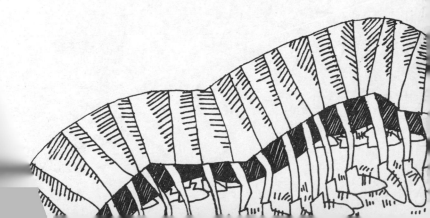

Chapter Eleven

When he pushed open the changing room door, the other children stopped talking and stared at him. Melanie Mayfly tugged her pigtails.

"What are *you* doing here?" she sneered. "Millipedes can't dance."

Everyone laughed, and Morris wanted to run back home. But he bit his lip and opened his eyes wide to stop himself crying. Then he began to lace up his shoes.

"What a slow-coach!" teased Melanie Mayfly. "The lesson will be finished before he's even dressed."

She stuck out her tongue at Morris and fluttered across to the mirror.

"Oh, aren't I pretty?" she sighed.

By the time Morris had put on four pairs of shoes, the others were ready, and they ran out of the changing room leaving him quite alone. He heard music; the lesson was starting without him, and he had 38 pairs of laces still to tie.

He tried to hurry, but his fingers wouldn't go any faster; they just got caught up in the knots. It was nearly half an hour before he was ready and he tiptoed timidly into the hall to join the class.

Chapter Twelve

The hall was high and wide, and all the walls were covered with mirrors. The children stood in lines facing Madame Butterfly, who sat at a very grand piano.

"You're late!" she snapped when Morris came in. But before he could explain about all the laces, she turned back to the class.

"Let me see you jump," she said.

Morris stared in dismay as the children leaped gracefully into the air, hovered on their wings, then landed gently on the floor. He'd *never* be able to do that. But he remembered the old Stag Beetle's words and tried his best. He jumped with his back end; he jumped with his front end; he jumped with his middle. But he couldn't jump with all of himself at once. It seemed that millipedes simply weren't designed for jumping.

"You'll have to do better than that," sighed Madame Butterfly.

But Morris couldn't do better. If only he had wings! If only he didn't have so many legs! It was a terrible start – but worse was to follow.

"Now let me see your spins," said Madame Butterfly.

The children stood on one leg, fluttered their wings and spun round in perfect circles. It wasn't even worth Morris trying.

He hung his head and crept out of the hall. He'd never come back, and his heart would never stop aching.

Chapter Thirteen

But that night, Morris dreamed of the old Stag Beetle and woke up feeling ashamed that he'd given up so easily. He *would* go back. He *would* try and try and try again. Let them laugh if they wanted to.

And he *did* go back. Oh, the other children giggled; Madame Butterfly sighed and snapped. But Morris took no notice. Each week he tried his hardest, and although he was still clumsy, he improved a little every time. And in the end, even Melanie Mayfly grew bored with laughing and left him alone.

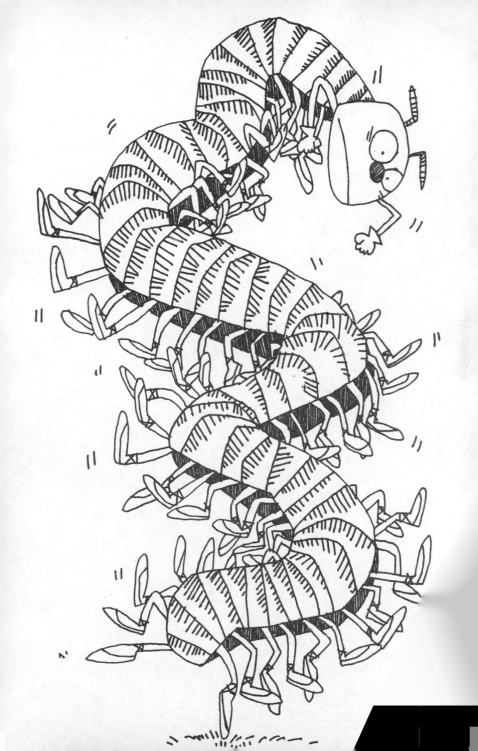

Chapter Fourteen

"Our Easter Concert is in four weeks' time," said Madame Butterfly one day. "We will be performing 'The Sleeping Beauty'. What a wonderful story! The Ugly Caterpillar sleeps in a cocoon for a hundred days, then turns into the Beautiful Butterfly."

Melanie Mayfly was to be the Beautiful Butterfly, of course, and Martin Moth was to be the Handsome Prince. Everyone else was given a part – everyone except Morris. As the others chattered excitedly, he coiled up sadly on his own in a corner. He'd tried so hard, but he wasn't good enough.

Madame Butterfly felt sorry for him. He was the worst pupil she'd ever had. But perhaps . . .

"Morris!" she called. "Come here. I have a part for you. I want you to be the Ugly Caterpillar."

Chapter Fifteen

Morris's part was small but very important. He had to spin across the stage into a huge silk cocoon; then Melanie Mayfly spun out of the other side as the Beautiful Butterfly. It was very difficult, and always made him dizzy. But he practised and practised until he could just about manage it.

Mrs Macmillipede made his Ugly Caterpillar costume, and all his family and friends bought tickets. As the concert drew near, Morris was so excited he couldn't concentrate at school. He was always in trouble with his teacher, Miss Louse.

Chapter Sixteen

Finally, the great day arrived. The lights in the hall went down; the audience fell silent; Madame Butterfly played the first notes on the piano; then the curtain rose and Martin Moth began the ballet.

Half an hour later, they reached the great moment when Morris had to spin into the cocoon. Madame Butterfly played loud and fast, and Morris spun out onto the stage. Everything went perfectly, and as he approached the cocoon, he began to think of the applause he'd soon receive. But that was a terrible mistake, for he stopped thinking about spinning. His front end began to spin faster than his back end, and his long, clumsy body coiled up like a spring.

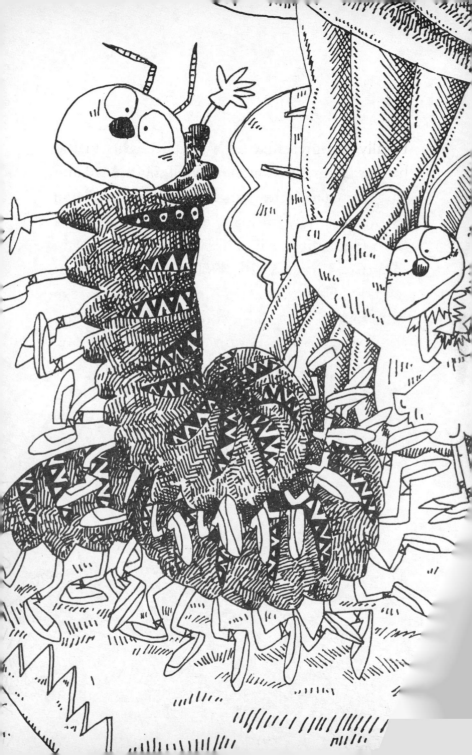

"Look out!" shouted Martin Moth.

Too late. The spring uncoiled and Morris whirled across the stage. He knocked Martin Moth into the piano; he knocked Melanie Mayfly into the audience; he knocked the scenery onto Madame Butterfly's head. Then he spun off stage and down the corridor, landing with a bump on the front steps of the school.

Chapter Seventeen

Morris had bruises everywhere, and his head wouldn't stop spinning. But the worst thing of all was the noise coming from inside – laughter. He'd made a fool of himself yet again.

He hurried away from the school and didn't stop until he reached the River Trickle. Leaning over Carrot Bridge, he stared down into the dark water. He was so miserable, he felt like throwing himself in. But he threw in his ballet shoes instead, all 42 pairs of them. They floated away into the night, taking Morris's dreams with them.

"Now, young man," said a gruff voice. There was the old Stag Beetle, puffing away at his pipe. "Tell me what happened."

Morris told him the whole story. "So you see, I really did try and try and try again."

"Indeed you did," agreed the Beetle. "But you see, my boy, millipedes just aren't made for ballet dancing. They have far too many legs."

Morris felt cross; if that was the case, why had the old man encouraged him?

"But now I know you don't give up easily, I'll tell you what millipedes are made for," said the Beetle.

Then he leaned over and whispered something in Morris's ear, so quietly you can't hear what he said. But it made Morris so happy, he clapped his hands and danced a jig round and round the old man.

Chapter Eighteen

Next evening, Morris went out after tea and came back two hours later with a great big grin on his face. When his mother asked him where he'd been, he just said, "You'll see." And he said the same thing every Thursday evening for the next six months.

One day, he came home and unrolled a bright yellow poster.

"What on earth are you up to?" asked his father.

"Just come and watch," said Morris.

"The last time we came to watch you," said his mother, "you were the laughing stock of Brussels Sprout."

But his parents agreed to come. And his brothers and all his friends bought tickets – they didn't want to miss Morris making a fool of himself again.

Chapter Nineteen

It was Saturday September 30th. The Macmillipedes drove to the theatre in their Ford Banana. What a crowd there was, all come to see Morris, all expecting to laugh at him.

At eight o'clock, the lights in the theatre went down, the curtain rose and there in a spotlight stood Morris, wearing a top hat and tails. What would he do?

The conductor raised his arms, the orchestra set off at a tremendous pace, and Morris began to . . . TAP DANCE!

Tap tap tap went his left foot T-t-t-t-t-tap went his right. T-t-t-t-t-t-t-tap. T-t-t-t-t-t-t-tap. T-t-t-t-t-t-t-t-t-t-t-tap. T-t-tap. T-t-tap. T-t-t-t-t-t-t-t-t-t-t-t-t-t-t-TAP.

The violinists' fingers flew; the pianist wished he had a hundred hands. But none of them could keep up with Morris the Miracle Macmillipede.

At the end of the show, the audience called and cheered and threw flowers. And best of all, not one person in the whole theatre laughed.

Chapter Twenty

There was a tremendous party in Morris's dressing-room that night; everyone wanted to be there to congratulate him.

"Well done!" said the old Stag Beetle. "You really did try and try and try again."

"You owe it to all those legs of yours," smiled the Beetle.

Morris's brothers and friends could hardly believe what had happened.

"We came to laugh," they said. "But we ended up cheering."

Madame Butterfly kissed him on both cheeks.

"Darling!" she breathed. "Didn't I always say you'd be a famous dancer one day?"

And Morris was feeling far too happy to remind her what she'd *really* said.

Chapter Twenty-One

Next morning, the newspapers were full of photographs of Morris, and the phone didn't stop ringing all day. Every theatre in the country wanted him to appear. Each time he danced, he was a huge success, and he was soon known as Morris Macmillipede, the Toast of Brussels Sprout. He was as rich as a bluebottle, and he bought a house in Celery Hills where all the famous stars live.

Nothing could have made him any happier. Or so he thought, until the day the telephone rang.

"Hello," said Morris.

"Oh, Mr Macmillipede, this is the Orange Crate Theatre. Dame Gossamer Spider is about to begin rehearsals for a new ballet, which has a most important part for a tap dancer. We were wondering ..."

AGENT Amelia

MICHAEL BROAD

Amelia Kidd is a secret agent, and her mission is to save the world. In fact, she's saved it loads of times from criminal masterminds. Read her secret case files, and find out all about it – available three in one book.

All £4.99

Ghost Diamond!
ISBN 9781842706626

Zombie Cows!
ISBN 9781842706633

Hypno Hounds!
ISBN 9781842708163

Spooky Ballet!
ISBN 9781842708170

Bobby and Charlton
stories by Sophie Smiley

with illustrations by
MICHAEL FOREMAN

Charlie's family are all football-mad. They always
work as a team, whether they have too much
snow, a fear of dogs, or are looking for a pirate
adventure. And the best player of all is Bobby,
who saves all the goals.

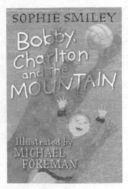

ISBN: 9781842701782

ISBN: 9781842704202

ISBN: 9781842706848

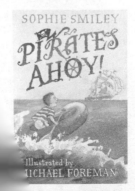

N: 9781842708828

ISBN:9781842708835

ISBN: 9781849390538

£4.99

DAMIAN DROOTH
SUPERSLEUTH

by Barbara Mitchelhill
with illustrations by Tony Ross

Detective work is Damian's thing, and he does solve all his cases, although he gets into an awful lot of trouble on the way! Read all the books and see how.

All £3.99

Disappearing Daughter
ISBN: 9781842705605

Popstar's Wedding
ISBN: 9781842705612

How to be a Detective
ISBN: 9781842705971

Spycatcher
ISBN: 9781842705674

Serious Graffiti
ISBN: 9781842706503

Dog Snatchers
ISBN: 9781842706497

Under Cover
ISBN: 9781842708255

Gruesome Ghosts
ISBN: 9781842708262

Football Forgery
ISBN: 9781849390354

JOE, LAURIE and THEO STORIES

by REBECCA LISLE

with illustrations by TIM ARCHBOLD

Theo has a dog with a very special collar, and the two of them find gnome burglars, a boy lost in a magic box and a boy in a bear pit – all with a great deal of help from older brothers Joe and Laurie, naturally!

All £4.99

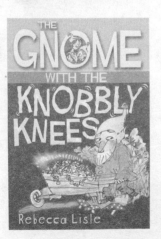

The Dog with the Diamond Collar
ISBN: 9781842703663

The Boy in the Big Black Box
ISBN: 9781842706817

The Gnome with the Knobbly Knees
ISBN: 9781842708897

Ms Wiz

by **TERENCE BLACKER**
with illustrations by **Tony Ross**

Ms Wiz always comes when Magic is needed, and Class Five
do test that in every way. After all, a paranormal operative is
a handy person to have helping out – whether it's arranging
class trips to tropical islands, or finding a lost cat.

**'Funny, magical . . .
with wicked pictures
by Tony Ross,
it's the closest
thing you'll get
to Roald Dahl.'**
The Times

All £4.99

ISBN: 9781842707029

ISBN: 9781842707036

ISBN: 9781842708477

ISBN: 9781842708484

ISBN: 9781842708583

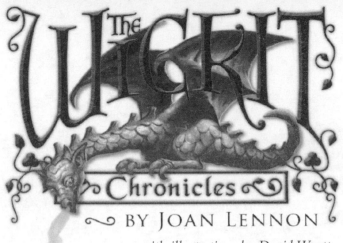

THE WICKIT Chronicles

BY JOAN LENNON

with illustrations by David Wyatt

Pip lives in a monastery in the middle of the Fens, but adventure finds him even there. He sings for the King at Ely, discovers an enemy army right in the Fens,

and even meets a Viking maiden. But best of all is his friend Perfect, a living stone dragon, who can fly and swim and breathe fire.

Ely Plot
ISBN: 9781842705957

Fen Gold
ISBN: 9781842706329

Ice·Road
ISBN: 9781842707708

Witch Bell
ISBN: 9781842708576

All £4.99